SCARY TALES RETOLD™

LITTLE DEAD RIDING HOOD

by Wiley Blevins • illustrated by Steve Cox

RED CHAIR
·PRESS·

Please visit our website at **www.redchairpress.com** for more high-quality products for young readers.

About the Author

Wiley Blevins has taught elementary school in both the United States and South America. He has also written over 70 books for children and 15 for teachers, as well as created reading programs for schools in the U.S. and Asia with Scholastic, Macmillan/McGraw-Hill, Houghton-Mifflin Harcourt, and other publishers. Wiley currently lives and writes in New York City.

About the Artist

Steve Cox lives in London, England. He first designed toys and packaging for other people's characters. But he decided to create his own characters and turned full time to illustrating. When he is not drawing books he plays lead guitar in a rock band.

Publisher's Cataloging-In-Publication Data

Blevins, Wiley.
   Little Dead Riding Hood / by Wiley Blevins ; illustrated by Steve Cox.

   pages : illustrations ; cm. -- (Scary tales retold)

   "Unlike the classic Grimm's tale told to children for centuries, our heroine never makes it past the Wolf in Grandma's clothing. In this grim retold tale, Little Dead Riding Hood joins forces with the Wolf to trap unsuspecting boys and girls deep in the forest."--Provided by publisher.
   Issued also as an ebook.
   ISBN: 978-1-63440-102-9 (library hardcover)
   ISBN: 978-1-63440-103-6 (paperback)

   1. Girls--Juvenile fiction. 2. Wolves--Juvenile fiction. 3. Girls--Fiction. 4. Wolves--Fiction. 5. Fairy tales. 6. Horror tales. I. Cox, Steve, 1961- II. Title. III. Title: Based on (work) Little Red Riding Hood.

PZ7.B618652 Li 2016
[E]   2015906802

Scary Tales Retold first published by:
Red Chair Press LLC   PO Box 333   South Egremont, MA 01258-0333

Printed in the United States of America
Distributed in the U.S. by Lerner Publisher Services. www.lernerbooks.com

0516 1 CBGF16

In a village long ago, there lived a little girl. She always wore a red hood. So the people in the village called her Little Red Riding Hood.

One day, the little girl went to visit her grandmother. She lived in a small hut in the forest. A hungry wolf put on her grandmother's clothes.

He tricked Little Red Riding Hood. Then the wolf ate her with one big CHOMP!

The people in the village thought that was the end of Little Red Riding Hood. But they were wrong.

Dead wrong.

One day, another little girl went into the
forest. She was there to pick flowers for
her mother.

As she bent down, she heard a noise.
It sounded like soft footsteps. A shiver, like a
hundred spiders, crawled up her back. Afraid
it was the wolf, she slowly turned to see . . .

A girl in a red hood. But instead of a face, she saw only two glowing red eyes. And glowing yellow teeth.

A voice like the wind whispered.
In the woods,
A red hood on my head,
I met the big wolf,
And now I'm dead.
Who will be next?

The little girl shot out of the forest.
She ran through the village screaming.
Everyone gathered to hear what had happened.

"The ghost of Little Red Riding Hood
warned me. She saved me from the wolf,"
the little girl said.

After that day, children who went into the forest sang a song to ask for Little Red Riding Hood's help.

Dead Riding Hood,
Dead Riding Hood,
Come out to play.
Dead Riding Hood,
Dead Riding Hood,
Keep the wolf away.

Over time, children got less afraid. One day,
a group of boys went into the forest to play.
The boys set out to build a huge fort.

"What about Dead Riding Hood?" asked the smallest boy.

The other boys laughed. "There's nothing to fear. Come. We need to get the sticks and stones for our fort."

So the boys went farther into the woods.
They spread out. In time, the smallest boy
could not see or hear the other boys. Just
then a voice like the wind whispered.

In the woods,
A red hood on my head,
I met the big wolf,
And now I'm dead.
Who will be next?

And there stood Dead Riding Hood.

"The wolf must be near," said the boy.
He raced toward the edge of the forest.
"No," moaned Dead Riding Hood.

"Then where should I run?" he asked. Dead
Riding Hood pointed deeper into the forest.

The boy ran as fast as his legs could carry
him. Around big rocks. Over little streams.
And into the darkest part of the woods.
There he came upon a large cave.

"Go inside," said Dead Riding Hood.

"I can hide from the wolf in there," said the boy. "Thank you." Then he slid into the dark, dark cave.

The boy looked around. A pair of glowing
red eyes stared back at him. Suddenly, he felt
something grab his arm. It dragged him to
the back of the cave. And there, beside a big
cooking pot, sat . . .

The wolf.

The wolf looked at Dead Riding Hood.
"You brought me such a tasty treat this time.
Good girl."

Dead Riding Hood smiled with her glowing
yellow teeth. Then she floated out of the
cave in search of another little boy or girl.

WHO WILL BE NEXT?

STORY
MICHAEL MORECI

ART
KYLE CHARLES

COLORS
MATT BATTAGLIA

LETTERS
RYAN FERRIER

®

image

IMAGE COMICS INC.

Robert Kirkman – Chief Operating Officer
Erik Larsen – Chief Financial Officer
Todd McFarlane – President
Marc Silvestri – Chief Executive Officer
Jim Valentino – Vice-President

Eric Stephenson – Publisher
Corey Murphy – Director of Sales
Jeff Boison – Director of Publishing Planning & Book Trade Sales
Jeremy Sullivan – Director of Digital Sales
Kat Salazar – Director of PR & Marketing
Branwyn Bigglestone – Controller
Sarah Mello – Accounts Manager
Drew Gill – Art Director
Jonathan Chan – Production Manager
Meredith Wallace – Print Manager
Briah Skelly – Publicist
Sasha Head – Sales & Marketing Production Designer
Randy Okamura – Digital Production Designer
David Brothers – Branding Manager
Olivia Ngai – Content Manager
Addison Duke – Production Artist
Vincent Kukua – Production Artist
Tricia Ramos – Production Artist
Jeff Stang – Direct Market Sales Representative
Emilio Bautista – Digital Sales Associate
Leanna Caunter – Accounting Assistant
Chloe Ramos-Peterson – Library Market Sales Representative

IMAGECOMICS.COM

DESIGN
TIM DANIEL